Listen and follow...

1 Scan the QR code using the camera on your phone or tablet. (You might need to download a QR reader first.)

2 Click on the link that pops up.

3 Press play to hear the story being read aloud.

4 Turn the page when you hear the twinkle!

First published 2019 by Twinkl Ltd.
197 Ecclesall Road, Sheffield S11 8HW

ISBN: 978-1-8381906-0-6

FSC
www.fsc.org
MIX
Paper from
responsible sources
FSC® C022913

We're passionate about giving our children a sustainable future, which is why this book is made from Forest Stewardship Council® certified paper. Learn how our Twinkl Green policy gives the planet a helping hand at www.twinkl.com/twinkl-green.

Printed in the United Kingdom.

10 9 8 7 6 5 4 3 2 1

A catalogue record for this book is available from the British Library.

Twinkl is a registered trademark of Twinkl Ltd.

A Monster Surprise

A TWINKL ORIGINAL

twinkl

Twinkl Educational Publishing

Beneath the leafy rooftop of the woods in Little Nook
Was a very hungry rabbit, who was searching by the brook.

"My **flowers** have been stolen – almost every single bunch!"
Rabbit panicked, feeling sure that there was not enough
for lunch.

He saw a clump of fur between some
sticks upon the ground
And he thought that he might know
just where the culprit might be found.

So, Rabbit marched to Squirrel's house
to find his precious food
And to tell his friend that taking it was
really rather rude.

"Excuse me!" shouted Rabbit, now with Squirrel in his sight. "I was really looking forward to my marigold delight.

I know you took my flowers. Please return them right away."

But it wasn't only Rabbit who was missing food that day.

"My **acorns** have been stolen!" Squirrel
shouted with a cry.
"And the villain left a bite mark in my
tree as they went by."

The friends knew just one creature who
would nibble on a tree
And they thought that they might know
just where the culprit might now be.

So, on they marched to Beaver's house to
find their precious food
And to tell their friend that taking it was
really rather rude.

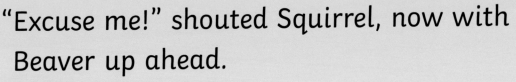

"Excuse me!" shouted Squirrel, now with Beaver up ahead.

"I was really looking forward to my toast with acorn spread.

I know you took my acorns. Would you kindly give them back?"

But it wasn't only Squirrel who was cross about her snack.

"My **branches** have been stolen!" snuffled
  Beaver, full of grief.
"And I'm sure I saw a pointy tusk belonging
  to the thief."

The friends knew just one creature with
a tusk of any sort
And they thought that they might know
just where the culprit might be caught.

So, on they marched to Boar's house, off to find their precious food
And to tell their friend that taking it was really rather rude.

"Excuse me!" shouted Beaver, now that Boar
was in her view.
"I was really looking forward to my branch
and bramble stew.

I know you took my branches and I'd like
them back, unchewed!"

But it wasn't only Beaver who was longing for her food.

"My **berries** have been stolen!" snorted Boar,
wide-eyed with shock.
"And the robber left some footprints leading
right across that rock.

I've never seen a creature who has
footprints of that kind
So I think that we should follow
them to see what we can find."

The friends climbed up the rock and clambered down the other side
As they trekked to find their food with just the footprints as their guide.

They took a narrow path that formed a line between the trees...

And then crawled through thorny
bushes that left scratches on their knees.

They climbed some jagged rocks
until their feet could take no more.

Then, they came across a cave that had a boulder for a door.

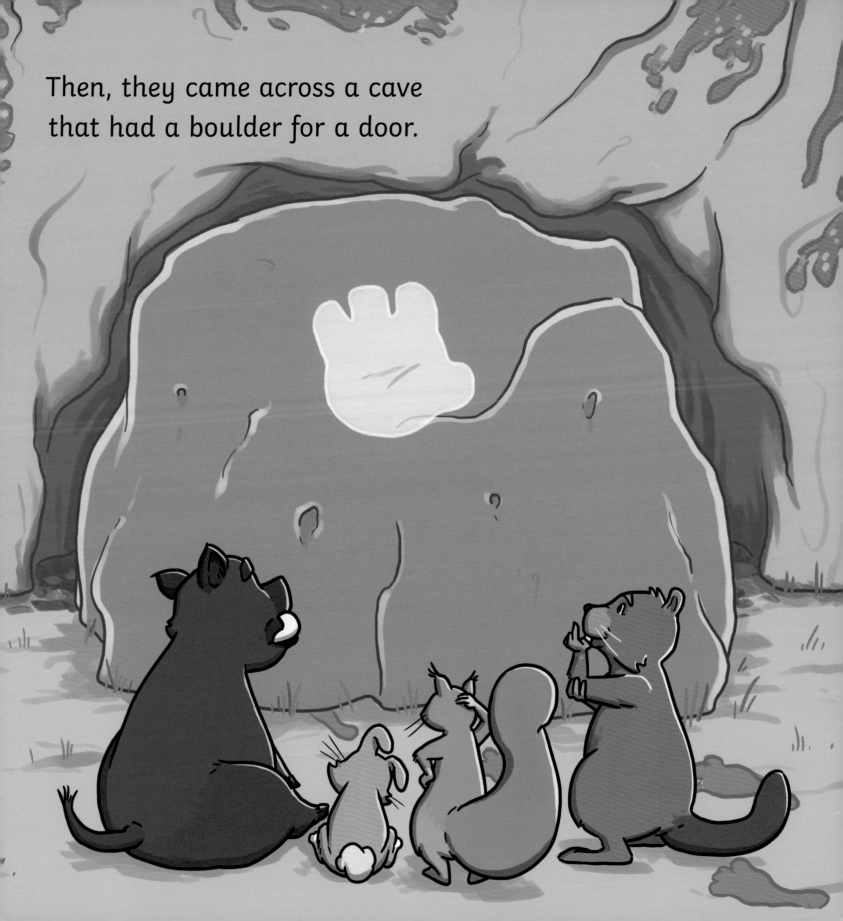

The boulder started moving and the creatures
stood in fright
As a silhouette inside began to shuffle into sight.

"A monster!" Rabbit shouted as the friends all
turned to flee.

In the panic, Rabbit tripped,
colliding head first with a tree.

The monster's hand loomed down and as it picked him up, he shook.
There was nothing quite so scary in the whole of Little Nook!

"Oh, please say you won't eat me!"
Rabbit begged with *fearful eyes*.

"I would **never** eat a rabbit!" laughed the monster with surprise.

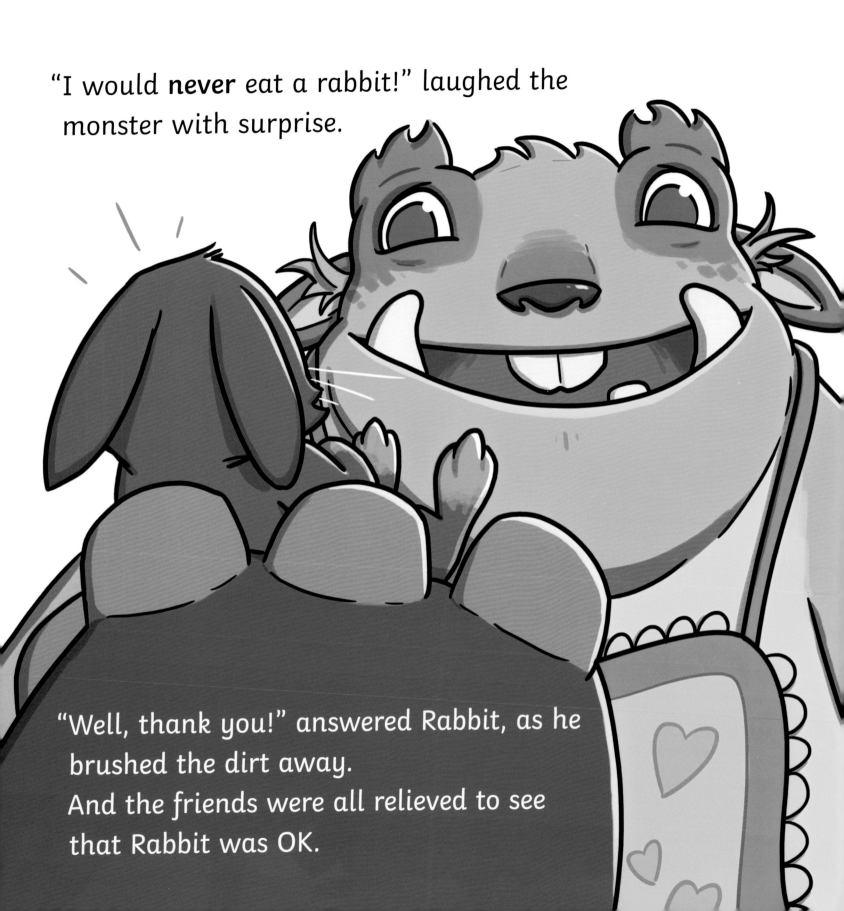

"Well, thank you!" answered Rabbit, as he brushed the dirt away.
And the friends were all relieved to see that Rabbit was OK.

The monster mumbled shyly as it
bent down on one knee,
"I was hoping that you all would
like to join me for some tea."

The monster clicked its fingers and the glow-worms shined their lights
On the most amazing party full of wonderful delights.

"Our missing foods!" said Rabbit, now the
monster's plan was clear,
And the creatures all said sorry for reacting
with such fear.

"Please join me," said the monster,
as it headed for the seats.
"You can help yourself to cups of tea
and lots of yummy treats."

When Rabbit's little tummy brimmed with marigold delight,
And when all the toast had gone with no more acorn spread in sight,

When Boar was full of berries and the stew was at an end,
They all thanked the gentle monster...

who was now their brand new friend.

Continue the learning with exclusive teacher-created resources to engage and inspire children at school, at home and beyond...

Visit **twinkl.com/originals**

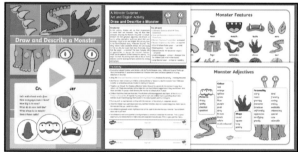

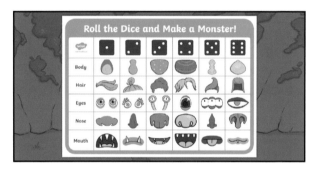

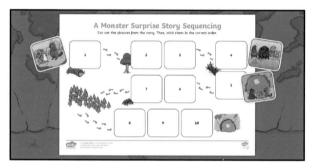

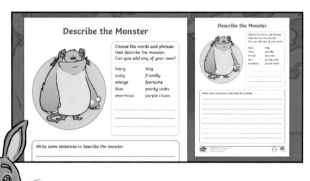

For accompanying teaching materials,
scan the QR code above or visit **twinkl.com/originals**

This Twinkl Originals book belongs to:

_____

_____